Tools at the Pool

By Marcy Kelman
Illustrated by Alan Batson

DISNEP PRESS

NEW YORK

DISNEP PRESS

First Edition 10 9 8 7 6 5 4 3 2 1
Library of Congress Cataloging-in-Publication Data on file
ISBN 978-1-4231-1769-8

Manufactured in the USA
For more Disney Press fun, visit www.disneybooks.com

"And the first caller to answer today's riddle correctly will win a weekend getaway to Relaxation Resort!"

"Listen, everybody," Felipe said excitedly. "Jack Stack is about to reveal today's Rockin' Radio Riddle."

"Okay, here's the riddle: what kind of driver never gets a speeding ticket?"

"I've got it!" shouted Felipe. "Quick, help me dial the phone!"
Rusty helped prop up the phone receiver for Felipe, while
Squeeze used a pencil eraser to dial the radio station's number.

"You're on the air with Jack Stack. Who's this?"
"This is Felipe, from Manny's Repair Shop!"
"Hey, there, Felipe. Do you know the answer?"
"¡Sí! The kind of driver that never gets a speeding ticket is a screwdriver!"
"That's correct! Congratulations, Felipe! You win the getaway to Relaxation Resort. I'll be delivering your prize in person after today's show."
The whole teamed cheered and jumped up and down.

Manny came out of the back room carrying a box of supplies. "What's going on? Are you guys throwing a *fiesta*?"

"Not yet, but you'll want to throw one when you find out what Felipe just won!" cheered Squeeze.

"What did you win, Felipe?" Manny asked.

"A weekend getaway to Relaxation Resort for all of us!" Felipe said proudly. "Isn't that *maravilloso*?"

Manny scratched his head. "Gee, I don't know…leave the shop for two days? Things can get awfully busy around here."

Dusty looked at the calendar. "But we don't have anything scheduled for this weekend!"

Manny felt a little uneasy. "Well, uh, what if something comes up, like an *emergencia*? Someone might need our help while we're away."

The tools thought hard. Then Stretch had an idea. "I know! We'll give your cell-phone number to Mr. Lopart, and he can call us if there's an emergency."

"Aw, come on, Manny," Pat pleaded. "Everyone needs some time off!"

"It's true!" said Felipe. "If anyone needs a vacation, it's Turner. Have you noticed how crabby he's been lately?"

"What do you mean?" Turner scowled. "I haven't been crabby lately!"

"You're right. It's not just lately—*it's all the time*!" Felipe laughed.

Manny smiled. "We *have* been working really hard lately, and it's important to take breaks. Maybe a weekend at Relaxation Resort is just what we need."

The tools all cheered! Just then, Jack Stack entered the shop.

"Hey, Felipe—my Rockin' Riddler of the day! Are you ready for a vacation that's sure to be a sensation?" Jack asked.

Felipe bounced up and down. "*Sí, estoy listo*! I'm ready!"

"Here's your gift certificate and a brochure all about the resort," Jack said.

The team gathered around Jack to look at the brochure.

"Ooh, they have a golf course, tennis courts, and a pool!" shouted Dusty. "Fun in the sun, here we come!"

That weekend, the team headed out. After a few hours on the road, they arrived at the resort.

"Wow!" Felipe gasped. "It has even more razzle-dazzle than I imagined!"

Manny inspected the entryway. "Hmm, there's a loose brick on this walkway. I should fix that in case someone trips. And the latch on this gate needs to be tightened."

"We're here to relax, not to work!" Turner reminded Manny. "That's what vacations are all about."

"Gee, you're right," Manny admitted. "I've got to stop thinking about repairs and just unwind. Come on, let's check out our room!"

RELAXATION RESORT

The tools were thrilled to be spending their very first night in a hotel room.

Stretch marveled at the beautiful room. "It's so glamorous!"

"And, look—there are chocolates on the pillow!" shrieked Dusty.

When Manny put his bag on the table, it wobbled. "Look at this *mesa*," he said.

Pat was puzzled. "What mess? This place is sparkling clean."

"Unplug your ears: Manny said *mesa*, not mess!" grumbled Turner. "*Mesa* means table in Spanish."

"W-w-what's wrong?" Rusty panicked. "Is the table going to topple over?"

"No, it's just wobbly," Manny explained. "But if we reinforce the joint in the front right leg, it will be as good as new!"

Felipe sighed. "No work allowed on vacation, remember?"

Manny shook his head and smiled. "You're right, Felipe. It's time to relax and enjoy this wonderful getaway. I'll just wash up before we go to the pool."

In the bathroom, Manny saw that the sink's faucet was dripping. "Hey, the *agua* is..." Manny's voice trailed off. He knew he had to get his mind off work. After all, this was the tools' first time in a hotel, and Manny didn't want to spoil it.

"Is something wrong, Manny?" asked Stretch.

"No, Stretch," answered Manny. "I was just going to say that I bet the *agua* in the pool is crystal blue. Let's go check it out!"

"Woo-hoo! All cool tools to the pool!" cried Squeeze.

The tools enjoyed themselves at the pool: Felipe danced to the radio; Turner read the newspaper; Rusty and Stretch played badminton; and Squeeze and Pat floated on the water.

Manny sat down in a lounge chair next to Dusty, put on sunscreen, and tried hard to keep his mind off repairs.

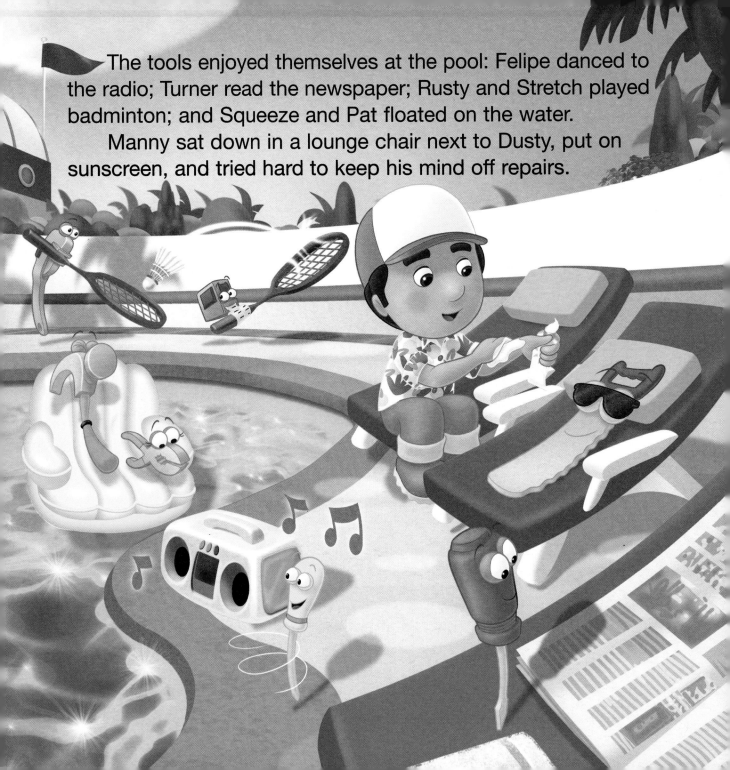

Just then, a little girl in the pool began to cry.

Felipe hopped over to her. "What's wrong, *señorita*?"

"My boat broke, and now my dolly can't cross the pool." The girl sobbed.

The girl's mother rushed to her side. "It's okay, Sally. Come on, let's get you out of the water."

As soon as Manny heard about the problem, he wanted to help. "Excuse me, ma'am. If you'd like, my tools and I would be happy to fix Sally's boat."

"Oh, we'd be so grateful for your help," Sally's mom said with relief. "The boat was a special gift from Sally's grandfather, and it means a lot to her!"

"*No problemo*," Manny said. "We'll have it fixed in a jiffy!"

Within minutes, the team had repaired Sally's boat. Sally didn't stop grinning for the rest of the day, and her mom was very thankful for Manny's help.

"Wow, Manny, this is the most relaxed I've seen you since we got here," noted Turner.

"Making repairs makes me happy. It feels good to help," explained Manny.

Squeeze laughed. "I guess fixing things really floats your boat, huh?"

"Maybe if you fixed all the problems you noticed here at the resort, you could get it out of your system," Stretch said.

Manny was surprised. "Wait a minute—what about relaxing by the pool and keeping my mind off work?"

Dusty chuckled. "A lot of good that was doing! Why don't we just fix the walkway brick, the latch on the gate, the wobbly table, and the leaky faucet you thought we didn't see, and then come back here to lounge by the pool?"

Everyone agreed on this plan, and the team jumped on the repairs.

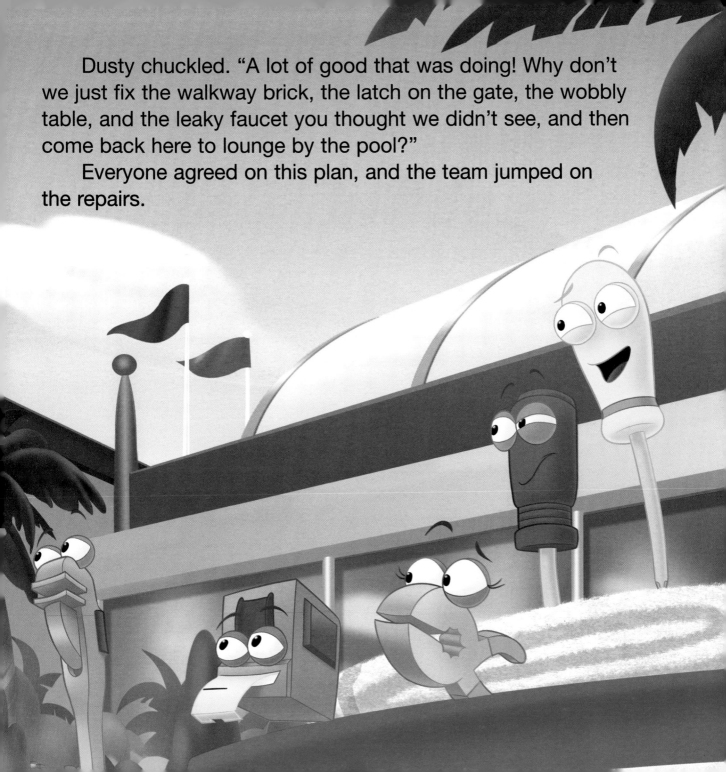

Before long, the repairs were finished. "Hey, where's Manny?" asked Rusty.

"Shhhhh," whispered Felipe. "He's sleeping like a log!"

"Yikes! It's not safe to sleep in the fireplace!" Pat panicked.

Squeeze giggled. "No, Pat. Manny's in bed, finally enjoying his vacation. No wonder they call this place Relaxation Resort!"

"Yeah, if you can't *relax*," snickered Turner, "you just *resort* to hard work—and you'll be fast asleep in no time!"